1 MONTH OF
FREE
READING

at

www.ForgottenBooks.com

ISBN 978-0-483-19430-4
PIBN 10801105

HEART STORIES

BY

JEAN BLEWETT

*Published under the distinguished patronage of
the Imperial Order Daughters
of the Empire.*

WARWICK BROS. & RUTTER
LIMITED   -   -   -   TORONTO

PS
8453
L48H5

THE Amelia F. Sim's Chapter Imperial Order of the Daughters of the Empire is deeply indebted to Mrs. Jean Blewett for permission to use the stories contained in this brochure, the proceeds from the sale of which are to be devoted to the fund for the blinded and to Chapter purposes.

MAXWELLTON

MAXWELLTON

MAXWELLTON

LITTLE Joe Morrison was making ready for Thanksgiving—so were all the Maxwellton people, for the matter of that—not the commonplace Thanksgiving as observed in less favored spots, but the real institution as inaugurated by the earliest Maxwellton settlers and kept up by their children's children to the third and fourth generation.

Why not? In all of Canada, the Maxwellton folks were convinced of it, there was not to be found a spot so fair, fruitful, and altogether desirable as their own neighborhood: therefore it was their fit, meet, and bounden duty to be grateful.

The Maxwellton Thanksgiving was part and parcel of the history of the place. It dated back to the days when the roads were trails, the farms big stretches of woods dotted with clearings so meagre they might have passed unnoticed but for the glow of burning brush heaps.

"God's care has kept us, His blessing been upon us as a people: as a people let us meet together and offer prayer and praise. We have no church as yet, but our valley is fair enough to worship in." So had spoken Joseph Morrison, whose upbringing had been in a strict Presbyterian household.

"Well thought of, Joe, and we women will take along our baskets, that when we are through with the singing and praying we may eat our dinner together on the green, and visit in a social way." So had answered him the wife of his bosom, of the Methodist persuasion, sunny and sweet as a briar rose.

"Ah, Jane, I'm afraid you link your religion and sociability so close together you can scarce tell one from the other." The dark eyes of him had smiled on her in a way which offset the reproof. "Our gathering will be for the purpose of returning thanks to the Father of Mercies."

"And of being happy together in a neighborly way," Jane had supplemented.

In the valley, nestling between two wooded hills, with the blue waters of Lake Ontario creeping up on the shore, Maxwellton kept its first Thanksgiving. In the valley it continued to be kept, and always the order followed was the same as on that first occasion, a service of praise followed by a friendly feast. The real harvest home, as Mrs. Morrison had remarked in the beginning of things, ought to be held in God's out-of-doors, where one has but to lift his eyes to see the yellow stubble and the stacks of grain. After awhile the valley

9

boasted a log church; later on a stone structure with a lofty spire, but this was not until these stalwart pioneers had worked the miracle of turning forest to field and meadow. Maxwellton became a prosperous, populous neighborhood, a progressive one as well. But one fashion changed not; as of old, in one day of each golden autumn men carried their Bibles and women their baskets to the valley between the hills.

To the old the day became, in a way, a sacrament, a thing set about with precious memories, beautiful in itself, more beautiful in its associations. To the young it continued to be a glorious combination of picnic and camp meeting.

Little Joe Morrison belonged to the last-named class. He was young, too young, he often thought. When a chap is a head taller than his own father, and overflowing with manly ambitions, it is a drawback to be but seventeen years of age. He was the youngest grandson of that Joe Morrison, who long before had inaugurated the Maxwellton Thanksgiving, and who was still alive and hearty, and young enough to be the bosom friend of his grandson. There were times when Little Joe felt a vague pity for himself and his ambitions.

It was hard to be six feet tall and yet be called Little Joe to distinguish him from his five-foot-seven father, known as Big Joe, and from his grandfather, Old Joe. Still it might easily have been worse— three Percivals in one house, or an equal number of Claudes, Alberts, or some such stuckup names. At least there was nothing flowery about Joe.

Little Joe's part in the general preparation had to do with the light waggon used by the Morrisons when they rode out in state. At the foot of the lane, where you turned into the pasture field, ran a creek, and in this creek just behind a great clump of elderberry bushes was the swimming hole in which it was his duty and pleasure to soak said waggon in the vain hope of silencing its spokes and tires. Had the time been April or early May, with the ice just gone and mosses showing green and yellow, he would have had most of the Maxwellton boys for company, but the normal youth has recovered from the swimming fever by the time summer has really arrived, and by the autumn has forgotten the symptoms. Little Joe did not mind. He had his brindle pup, and inquisitive blackbird, and his own pleasant thoughts for company—and to-morrow was the outing of the year! He gave the waggon plenty of time. In the morning his mother could settle her plump figure on the spring seat and inquire: "Has the rig been soaked?" Being answered in the affirmative, every trace of anxiety would fade from her face. Little Joe loved her face, was certain it was prettier than Mrs. Hays', Mrs. French's, Aunt Maria Lock's or Miss—no, not prettier than the new schoolma'am's. She—he had reached that stage when the school ma'am meant "she"—had curly hair, eyes that laughed at you, a gold filling in a front tooth and wore a back comb set with shiny bits of beads. For two cents, he told himself, the pup and the rusty black bird teetering on the elder bush, "I'd invite her to ride to meetin' in our rig."

Blushing and chuckling at his own temerity, he drew the light waggon up, then dumped it back into the swimming hole with a force which threatened to break a spring. "It's one of two things," the blackbird cocked his head knowingly. "To-morrow I get fun enough to last me the year or I waste my day." He hoped nothing would turn up to interfere with the holiday; he also hoped his mother would not get talking about Ed. at breakfast, and cry into her teacup, like she did Christmas and Easter. He was sick of hearing plaints about the absence of his oldest brother. If Ed. was too busy having a good time and making money to come and see the folks, why let him. Who cared? Not Joe—only when his mother's eyes filled up and ran over, as they often did, he always forgot the dignity supposed to hedge his seventeen years, and cried, too. It was aggravating. Ed. might write anyway. A picture postcard cost only a cent, and held only a line. Ed. might do that much for the credit of the family.

Parliament had nothing to do with fixing the date of Maxwellton's Thanksgiving. It was held year after year on the first Thursday of September, and there was an unwritten law to the effect that nothing short of a funeral should interfere with it. Births and marriages did not count, and so far nobody had been inconsiderate enough to die during this particular week—that is, nobody but old man Jarvis, and he had not had all his faculties for quite a while. Little Joe recalled to mind that it had not hurt the gathering any. The old man had died Tuesday morning and been buried Wednesday afternoon. The whole Jarvis connection, not feeling like taking up the daily grind right on the heels of a funeral, had turned out at the Thanksgiving in stronger force than ever before.

Last year when Dr. Walters tried to scare the Taits out of going by telling them young Jamie was sick enough to die Mrs. Tait went calmly on making cream pies. She said if it came to the worst there was no place Jamie would rather die than at the Thanksgiving dinner. Jamie didn't die—boys didn't die, not often; they grew into men, owned farms, lost their hearts to pretty—this time the old waggon found the lowest depths of the swimming hole and the blackbird in his curiosity to find out what all the splashing meant nearly teetered himself off the elderberry bush. Presently Little Joe, after apostrophizing the rig as "a gay old Noah's ark gone shipwrecked," brought it to the surface and up on the bank. While it dried off he cut across the meadow, and perched himself on the townline fence in time to intercept the young, extremely young, teacher on her way home from school.

"You'll sure be at the meeting to-morrow," trying to speak carelessly and failing because the girl's smile brought her dimples into play, and the dimples made Little Joe realize that he could not be properly thankful if she were not present. "Folks would have fits if the schoolma'am didn't show up. They'd think you wasn't half thankful for the privilege of livin' in these parts. Git out, Rover! Sho! He's muddied your frock. That's good of you. I'm 'fraid you're too soft-hearted, you'll spoil the kids—say, when you laugh that way you look like a kid yourself. If I was learning my letters in the old red schoolhouse I wouldn't be scared of you. Go 'long! Where'd you find your men, I'd like to know? Not many big girls showing up for lessons to-day, eh? They're home helping ma cook up for Thanksgiving. I'm not eating a thing to-day; saving up. Notice how pale I am?"

The schoolma'am, with a smile which gave Little Joe a tantalizing glimpse of the gold filling and the dimples. said something about his freckles, and then, by way of putting personalities aside, inquired if Thanksgiving were a church affair.

"Church affair!" returned Joe, with unction. "I should say so— Methodists, Presbyterians, two kinds of Baptists, and Kellys. Well, so long, if you must go."

The day itself was worth while being thankful for—a blue and gold day such as we get only in the autumn. Old Joe, leaning against the barnyard fence, shading his eyes with a wrinkled hand, made the remark to Big Joe, who in turn passed it on to Little Joe, that it was just such a day as the one on which the first Maxwellton Thanksgiving had been observed.

"I took the Bible, and grandma the cheesecakes and chicken pie. Grandma said 'be sociable' "—his voice shook and the tears came into his dim blue eyes—"and she knew best, bless her!"

He missed grandma with her warmth of heart, her soft friendliness, her laughter; always he missed her, but most of all on this anniversary. Little Joe made a race for the stable, grabbed the harness off its peg, and charged at King and Prince with it. It was bad enough to have ma crying bright and early Thanksgiving morning without grandpa getting started. Why couldn't everyone be jolly?

Big Joe stood on tiptoe to lay his hand on his father's shoulder a rare show of affection in a Morrison.

"Ma's out of all the care and trouble. She's having a better time in heaven than we could give her here," he said, and the faith thrilling through his voice made the worn old words seem new and wonderful and strangely precious.

"I know, I know," a trifle impatiently, "but I can't get over missing her; she was such company. Your woman is good as gold—nobody thinks more of Lizzie than I do—but she can't. come up to your ma. There was four of the Martin girls, and Old Joe Morrison got the prettiest and sweetest of 'em—only he wasn't Old Joe then. I wish one of your girls looked like her, but," crossly, "they're both like Lizzie, and the boys take after you."

"Exceptin' Edward," put in Big Joe, softly.

"Sure enough," agreed the old man. He's got ma's eyes and smile and coaxin'. ways. That's one reason I miss him more than I would anybody else. I want him home, Joe."

"So do I." Big Joe spoke cheerfully, a trifle too cheerfully. "And so does Lizzie. His ma's feeling so hurt about him staying away from home for two whole years she can't get over it."

"What's keeping him?" demanded Old Joe. "What's holding Eddie away from us all?"

"Love of money." There was no bitterness in the words, only a great disappointment. "He wasn't satisfied to work the farm with me, so I gave him his share and let him go. After he went in business with Landry—you warned him of Landry all right—he hadn't a thought for anything but getting rich. Doesn't even write any more since he and his precious partner moved to Chicago. I don't mind for myself, but I hate to see his ma losing sleep over him."

"A sort of respectable prodigal son," said Old Joe, with some heat. "I'm 'shamed of him."

"He has to learn his lessons. Some day he'll know better."

"Yes, some day he'll come home to the fatted calf, and all the rest of it, and his old grandpa will see him while he's yet a great way off, and go out and give him a tongue-thrashing he won't forget in a hurry. You'll see. I've no patience with the young fool," and Old Joe, forgetting his grief for grandma in his wrath for the respectable prodigal of the Morrison flock, limped out to help Little Joe hitch the team to the light waggon.

Already down the townline, over the hill road, round by the lake shore went a string of vehicles, buggies, carts, carriages, waggons, bear-

13

ing men and women, lads and lassies, babies and baskets. The sunshine raced the procession to the valley, and a west wind, warm as a breath of summer, wound the blue mist about the hill as a child winds a ribbon about a spool.

"What's keeping ma?" Little Joe was impatient to be off. The Thompsons—and it was with them the schoolma'am boarded—had just driven past. "If there's anything I hate it's to start late and take everybody's dust."

"She'll be along. Doesn't want to go till after the ten train has gone through," Big Joe answered pacifically. "Don't you go hustling or fluttering ma. She's as touchy as a hen that's lost a chick. Poor ma!"

A chair was brought out from the kitchen, and with the help of his son and grandson Old Joe was mounted upon it, and from thence conveyed to the spring seat.

"No sign of anyone coming, eh?" he inquired as he settled himself and found a comfortable position for his rheumatic leg. "If Edward did put in an appearance——"

"Edward didn't come, pa," spoke up Mrs. Morrison, who had joined the others. Her voice was listless, her expression listless, her face pale and troubled. "I—I—if the rest of you don't mind I'll stay home and look after things. That's you; make a fuss!" as Little Joe exclaimed against such a proceeding. "It doesn't matter that I feel limp as a dish rag."

"Come along, ma," urged her husband. "Folks will be thinking Eddie has done something to be 'shamed of, and—that's right. Joe, you get in 'longside your ma, and drive. The girls'll come with grandpa and me and help look after the baskets. Now we're off."

"Wait," cried Old Joe, suddenly. "Stop the horses. My old eyes aren't too dim to see my own boy loping along the concession yonder. That's Ed.," excitedly; "that's him; let me out."

Then a queer thing happened, for, whereas it had taken a kitchen chair to elevate him to the spring seat, he made the descent alone and unaided. He was off to meet and welcome the Morrison prodigal, the boy with the eyes, the smile and the sunny ways of the dear, dead woman.

So it came to pass, just as Little Joe had feared all along, that the Morrisons were the very last to start for the grove. It was good to see Edward, even if he were looking sort of troubled, good to hear his voice, even if it did have a tremor in it; to know he was back from the big, wicked city, even if he was, as he'd whispered to grandfather Joe, "poor as Job's turkey." Everybody had to fuss over him, tell him

14

things. You know how it is when the boy of the house comes home.

"I've come back to work the farm," said Edward, after he had shaken hands with the men folks, kissed his sisters and held his mother to his heart. "I—I wasn't smart enough for the city sharks. I've been an awful fool."

Old Joe allowed himself to be lifted bodily to the spring seat. "We've all been fools in our day," he said, with cheerful finality, and a great peace settled over the whole Morrison clan.

"Ed. can drive if he likes," cried Little Joe in a spirit of self-sacrifice. "I don't mind."

But Ed. did not care to drive. He sat next his mother, and under cover of the linen spread held her hand all the way to the valley. He sat next her through the beautiful service, the prayers, the songs of praise. Oh, it was good to be back with his own folks—honest folks, clean, wholesome country folks!

It was a long service; at least Little Joe thought it long. He wished the faithful would not insist on giving their testimonies in detail. Still they were interesting, these testimonies, more so than any mere story could be. There was grandpa now getting to his feet. Little Joe sat up and listened intently. He tried not to look important, but he knew —none better—that grandpa was not only the finest looker, but the finest speaker in Maxwellton. Even the giddiest youngster lent a willing ear when grandpa spoke. He made heaven seem a nice big home, and God a father who looked after everybody and took care of everybody. By-and-bye he would go back to old days and old meeting times; he always did, and his voice would get soft and trembly, like the low notes of the church organ. The women would put their handkerchiefs to their eyes—they always did—so would the men; all but Mr. Hossack. He would put that useful article to his nose and there would be a mighty snorting. Why did old folks cry when they got together? What was grandpa saying?

"Seasons of joy and of sorrow come to mind. It has not been all hard. We've had our good times together as neighbors; been glad over the birth of a first-born; the seeing our sons and daughters choose the better part; the lifting of a mortgage from the homestead; the gathering in of a plentiful harvest—these and many more precious hours of joy we have shared together by the blessing of God; and as to the sorrow, we've shared it, too; shared the dark hours of lost faith, lost courage, lost happiness; shared the watching by the sick bed, the stiller watching by the dead; gone together to God's acre—that fairest spot in all Maxwellton—to lay our nearest and dearest down to sleep"—

there was a sob in grandpa's voice—"and God has gone with us, come back all the lonely road to our lonely home with us, kept and comforted us. Are they not precious to look back upon, those days that are past, precious to hold in memory, precious to talk over with the young of our neighborhood? We've lost some things we fain would have kept" —his eyes fell compassionately on Caleb and Martha Graham, who had lost an only son in action the year before—"we've had to let go of some of the best things of life, but we've kept hold of enough to make us rich, of our love for one another, our good desires, our honesty and truth. It has been worth while, friends, well worth while. Life's day grows brief with some of us; the other world draws so near that almost we can hear the voices of the ones that wait to greet us lovingly there as they greeted us lovingly here. Thank God for His tender mercies, His keeping care, and His patience; above all, for His patience."

> "Then let your songs abound,
>   And every tear be dry;
> We're marching through Emmanuel's ground
>   To fairer worlds on high."

Little Joe wondered if it were because most of the voices had a tremble in them that the singing was the sweetest he had ever heard, or was it that the pretty schoolma'am was leading. He swallowed the lump which had threatened to choke him, and joined in. He was glad the schoolma'am had heard grandpa speak, and, yes, glad that her eyes were a little red. Somehow her tears seemed such a beautiful tribute to grandpa's eloquence. She did not know, of course—it was a family secret—that ages and ages ago grandpa had started out to be a minister. There hadn't been money enough to—but this was another family secret.

It **was** a memorable Thanksgiving service, but he was not sorry when it ended, and his ma and the neighbor women began their labors. Maxwellton's menu had long been the boast of the countryside, and this one did not come a whit behind its predecessors. Each housekeeper had done her best, and this meant something among such women as Maxwellton boasted. The sandwich had not come into vogue there. The hams went to the table brown and spicy as to exterior, pink and sweet as to interior, but there was no great demand for them so long as the turkey held out, and it held out a good while, to say nothing of the roast ducklings with apple sauce and the brown-crusted chicken pies. There were jams, jellies and pickles, tarts which melted in the mouth, doughnuts which only old Miss Thomson knew the recipe for, storey cakes—and if you have not been at a country feast and seen the

16

storey cake in all its glory, the bottom storey baked in a large milk pan, the next in a smaller milk pan, the next in a two quart basin, and so on to the peak of crumbling fruit and sweetness—you have missed something, let me tell you. There were six of these cakes; Little Joe counted them. He also noted with keen delight that the ancient rivalry between the Lake Shore and Townline women in the matter of delicacies of every sort had brought about a consummation devoutly to be wished.

After dinner, while his pa, with the other men, sat and talked about the crops, and his ma told the neighbor women all about Edward's hard luck, and how he was going to work the south fifty on shares; how tickled he was to get home, and how tickled she was to have him. Little Joe hitched the fat farm horses to the light waggon, stuck his cap firmly on his shock of red hair, behind the hazel hedge where none could see, gave his team a touch of the whip and swept down in fine style on a group of young people.

"I'm taking Jack Barker and the Dillworth girls down the point for a drive." He addressed his remarks to the schoolma'am. "And I want you to come along. Now don't go hanging back," coaxingly, "for I'm countin' on it. That's right."

The school ma'am put one little foot on a rickety spoke, the other on the high step, and landed beside him. It seemed too good to be true.

"You are very kind to a stranger," she said, with a blush and smile.

"Stranger nothing!" with bashful gallantry.

"The others—oh, we'll pick 'em up out at the beach; then go down the point and have our pictures pulled."

"But at four the Baptist minister is going to give us a little talk on what we have to be thankful for," she expostulated.

"Sho! I know what I've got to be thankful for without being told, don't you, Emily?"

By which you will perceive that if any Maxwellton youth was wasting his day that youth was not Little Joe Morrison.

LOVE PAYS THE SCORE

LOVE PAYS THE SCORE

A NYHOW the papers call you a hero," said the comrade who had guided Jim to his gate and was now turning back. "A hero is a mighty nice name, Dan."

"Coward I am," muttered Dan. "Think of never setting eyes on a field of growin' grain, a lilac bush in flower, a strawstack afore the rain has took the honey colored shine out of it."

"Ay, and of the faces over——" began the other, but Dan's hand fell on his shoulder with a grip that hurt.

"Stop right there—I—I didn't dast to think o' never seeing folks. Things are as far as I can go—yet. Good-bye, and thanks, old pard."

None of Dan's own people met him at the Station for the reason that he had been at pains to keep the day of his arrival secret. He did not want to be met, welcomed, wept over—Lord no! It seemed only yesterday he had marched away gallantly, gaily, with the crowd cheering and the school children singing with might and main.

"The old Church bells will peal with joy
You're welcome home my own dear boy.
When Johnny comes marching home again.
Hurrah! Hurrah! Hurrah!"

And now with a heart as filled with bitterness as his world with blindness, he was burrowing his way like the mole he had become, back to the place ever waiting for the poor fellow who has come to the end of the road; home, the inn that keeps no tally, exacts no reckoning, and where sign (although invisible) reads: "This is Home, where Love keeps the score; this is the Inn of the Open Door."

He felt his way up the three worn steps and put a trembling hand on the knob. The thing dreaded most, since that day in hospital, when he had been told by the kindly young surgeon that the wound had destroyed the sight of both eyes, was upon him. He opened the door and stumbled in.

"Young Dan'el!" was all his father said, but it was enough. It is when we are old and wise that we use love in our thoughts rather than our words, lest a breath of its beauty or its pricelessness be wasted.

His wife, such a girl she was still, cried, "Oh, honey boy!" You may not believe it, but it is true as gospel that no other greeting could have held so much as those three silly words—at least to this pair.

21

She had said them when giving him his good-bye kiss, also with tears. But she was not crying now. Her low crooning laughter as she held him close ought to have taken the tang of bitterness out of Dan's soul—but did not. Never to see the rose of her cheek, the glow of her eye, the soft glad smile of her. Never to look into the wrinkled face of that old man by the hearth, never to——

"Put out your arms—Daddy," his wife interrupted, pushing him into a chair. "Here's a personage must have his innings first of all—two years old, Dan, and you've never seen him."

"Nor ever will see him," with a groan.

"He's not dark like us folk, Dan'el," the old man was saying. "His eyes are the color of the sky when it shines down in the blue water, and his hair is yaller as wheat ready for sickle." Do you guess whom he is like to? Your mother Dan'el. Oh, but he's the image of that dear, dead woman! Dost remember her, Dan'el?"

"Dad—Dad—Dad!" Proud boy, showing off his latest accomplishment, and making quite free with his new-found parent. "Dadda!"

"Dear God, just to see him!" poor Dan cried under his breath as he strained the dancing child to him. "Just one look to do me for a lifetime!"

Boy's dimpled fists beat upon his father's cheeks boisterously, joyously, his gaze fastened on the bandage covering his father's eyes. He scented a game of "I Spy," pulled said bandage off with a whoop of delight and patted, oh, so tenderly, the poor hurt eyes.

It is hard to set down in black and white the working of a miracle, but we must do it, for though wise men would have it that the restoration of sight to Dan was accounted for on scientific grounds, that, in fact, his blindness was not the permanent character ascribed to it by the young surgeon, to one small group it was, is and ever will be a miracle—love's own miracle.

The frightened Sadie, having carried Boy to his grandfather, was no time at all putting the bandage back. "Heaven grant he has not hurt you Dan dear!" she cried, and started in alarm as her husband jumped up and began capering awkwardly about the room.

"Oh, folks!" he cried. "That's some boy! I saw him. I saw him with my own eyes. The Lord has let me wash in the pool of Siloam like that other poor devil. I can see."

"You're sure you didn't imagine it, Dan dear?" 'Sadie's face was white with excitement; her hands white from pressure.

"Imagine nothing!" Dan's tone was jubilant. "He's got a curl like a drake's tail at the back of his head and his mouth's red and there's jam on his chin, and—oh, I've seen him once if I never see him again." He collapsed in a chair, and Sadie knelt beside him.

"Since you've seen him once, you are sure to see him always," she cried comfortingly.

THE LITTLE REFUGEE

THE LITTLE REFUGEE

THE wood fire burned itself into a pile of white ashes on the hearth. The room grew chilly and quiet—too quiet. "Christmas is almost here," I began, "what'll we kill?" I winced on the last word. I hadn't meant to say it, but a man isn't like a woman, he can't be always thinking and guarding.

"There is no Christmas in our heart, why should there be in our home? We will not keep the day." If mother had cried or put her little hand in my big one, or shown any feeling, it wouldn't have seemed so bad. I stared at her through the dusk. She used to be a soft, gentle woman, gentle in her ways, her moods, her expression. But since we had heard that our son Bobby, our only child, had given his life for his country, she had been like this, hard and bitter.

Mother was of Quaker descent. She hated war. There was nothing good about it. It was an abomination. No Red Cross enthusiasm touched her, no patriotic wave ever swept her along with it. She sat in the Chair of Judgment. War was a scourge let loose upon the world to give men an outlet for wicked ambitions, hate, lust of power and possessions. I had heard it over and over again. There was no such thing as just cause for war. Nations fought, but not for right; there was nothing right about it. Oh, the waste of life! The nations took the sons that mothers risked life to bring into the world, took and wasted them for gain of territory, for revenge, for a prouder name and place. Heaven forgive the waste and wickedness!

What made this outlook of mother's harder to put up with was the fact that she was such a dear thing. There was nobody like her, and yet here we were, getting farther apart every day. I'd been hoping that Christmas would help us, and now we weren't going to keep Christmas. She had said so, and she generally meant what she said.

At bedtime I prayed, as usual, that Britain would have plenty of men and munitions, and go in to a glorious victory. Mother rose from her knees and looked at me with unfamiliar, hostile eyes.

"How dare you approach God with this matter? It is all cruel, and evil, and wasteful of love and life."

She pressed her cheek, beginning to show beautiful lines and wrinkles, until the dent remained. "How can you, a Christian, uphold war?" she demanded.

Something stirred in my bosom and all my fear of hurting her fell away. "Hurrah for Britain!" I cried. "God save the King!"

"My child—she would not say "our"—"sacrificed for nought," she began, but I broke in:

"Nay, to save some other mother's child from worse than death. It is for this our soldiers fight."

"I know what I know," she answered, and now her face was so sad I wanted to kiss it, only that there seemed a gulf of misunderstanding between us.

The silence which fell was broken by a knocking on the door. Mother and I looked at each other in a queer sort of fright.

"Open!" came a voice—we both heard it, knew it, answered to it, as we had done for long enough—the voice we had not thought to hear again.

Although I was shaking, my hand was steady enough to draw the bolt and pull Bobby in. Yes, it was Bobby sure enough, or rather a nice, boney skeleton of Bobby, and he carried a child wrapped in a cloak. He spoke to his mother first, as was natural, asking her help, as was natural, for he held his burden out with:

"Take him, mother; he's a little Belgian boy. That's it, hold him to your breast while I get him some milk." I stared from the child back to Bobby, and thanked heaven for them both.

"I'll tell you about things after a while. Just now it's up to us to tend this wee laddie—he's nearly done out. I shouldn't have pushed on home to-night, but I wanted to see you—couldn't wait—good old dad!"

The child seemed to put everything else into the background. The one important matter for the moment was whether that little four-year-old bit of bloodlessness would take the milk and live or reject it and die. He looked as though he could die without half trying.

He took it. Something lighted mother's face like a flash of sunshine. "The darling," she whispered, and held him close. "The little man!" Bobby's arm slipped around her. "The smallest refugee of the lot. I've brought him home to you, mammie. I want him——."

"Yes," she prompted.

"I want him to show you, as only he can show you, why Britain went to war. He's the reason. Can't you see, mammie?"

Mother's look would have been stern, only that she had not been able to push the gladness out of it. Bobby was drawing off the heavy cape from the child.

I saw an awful horror grow in mother's face. I heard her white lips murmur: "One little hand has been severed at the wrist—oh! Oh!"

"Yes, and the little body is scarred with bayonet wounds—see," said Bobby, exposing a thin back, a poor, pitiful back. Mother cried out one word, a bad word—no, not so much a bad word as a strong one, but I'll not put it down. I don't believe the recording angel will either.

"If you saw a brutal man using a little child as this one has been used, what would you do, mother?" Bobby queried.

"Can you ask?" she sobbed. "I'd strike him to the earth."

"Just what we mean to do," he told her, with a smile. "You won't begrudge your boy when he's well enough to go back to the front, will you, mammie?"

Mother, the mutilated lad in her arms, stood up as if taking part in a sacrament. "God bless Great Britain! I—I didn't know she fought for this," her tears falling on the face of the Belgian child. Then, in spite of, or maybe because of, her Quaker blood, she went on in a voice that made me forget the years and thrill like a lad-lover: "I would give a dozen sons if I had them to give!"

By which token I knew that mother's eyes were wide open at last—also that we would keep Christmas.

Warwick Bro's & Rutter, Limited,
Printers and Bookbinders, Toronto, Canada.

Lightning Source UK Ltd.
Milton Keynes UK
UKHW050649111118
331957UK00027B/170/P